CONTENTS

CHAPTER 1
RUDE AWAKENING 6

CHAPTER 2
ON A RAMPAGE 19

CHAPTER 3
TO THE RESCUE 31

CHAPTER 4
CALM BEFORE THE STORM 43

CHAPTER 5
FIRE AND FURY 54

Years ago in a distant galaxy, the planet Krypton exploded. Its only survivor was a baby named Kal-El who escaped in a rocket ship. After landing on Earth, he was adopted by the Kents, a kind couple who named him Clark. The boy soon discovered he had extraordinary abilities fuelled by the yellow sun of Earth. He chose to use these powers to help others, and so he became the guardian of his new home.

DC
SUPER
HEROES

SUPERMAN

AND THE
TOXIC
TROUBLEMAKER

WRITTEN BY
LAURIE S. SUTTON

ILLUSTRATED BY
LEONEL CASTELLANI

SUPERMAN CREATED BY
JERRY SIEGEL AND JOE SHUSTER
BY SPECIAL ARRANGEMENT WITH THE JERRY SIEGEL FAMILY

Raintree is an imprint of Capstone Global Library Limited, a company incorporated in England and Wales having its registered office at 264 Banbury Road, Oxford, OX2 7DY – Registered company number: 6695582
www.raintree.co.uk
myorders@raintree.co.uk

Designed by Brann Garvey

978 1 3982 0609 0

British Library Cataloguing in Publication Data
A full catalogue record for this book is available from the British Library.

Printed and bound in the United Kingdom

CHAPTER I

Rude awakening

BLEEP! BZZZZ! WHIRRRRR!

High-tech scientific equipment beeped, buzzed and whirred as two scientists prepared for an experiment. They were hard at work in an underground S.T.A.R. Labs facility not far from Metropolis.

"Are you sure it's safe to be doing this?" Dr Michaels asked his partner. "It sure doesn't look safe."

"Relax. It's safe. The monster is sleeping," replied Dr Frank. "He's been that way ever since the Justice League captured him and brought him here."

They stood in front of a super-villain with a limited mind named Chemo. The creature was a giant green blob of toxic chemicals held together by a clear, flexible plastic skin. Chemo's body had a human shape, but he was not human at all. Metal bands with round lenses covered his face where his eyes were supposed to be. He had a mechanical mouth. His hands looked like robot claws. Big metal boots covered his feet.

"I'm just glad he's napping," Dr Michaels said. "Otherwise I'm not sure we'd be able to keep him restrained. If he wakes up, he'll be running all around S.T.A.R. Labs in a mindless rage in no time."

The enormous super-villain was strapped to a wall by large metal clamps and was hooked up to a web of wires and sensors. Computer monitors showed symbols, numbers and other information that only the scientists understood.

"I don't know how Chemo can even be alive," Dr Frank said in amazement. "He doesn't have a heartbeat or any brainwaves. He isn't breathing."

"The files say that he started out as a simple vat of chemical waste," Dr Michaels said. "A lab accident brought him to life."

"Yes, but no one knows what was in that chemical waste. No one knows what's inside of him now," Dr Frank said. "If we can figure that out, we can make an 'anti-Chemo' formula to shut him down once and for all. Sort of like an antidote for a poison."

"That's why it's our job to get a sample of the liquid inside of him," Dr Michaels said. "We have to identify the chemicals."

"But first we need to get through Chemo's flexible skin. I've never seen anything like it," Dr Frank said.

The scientist pressed his finger against Chemo. It was like pushing against very thick cling film. The gooey liquid inside the creature moved a little bit, then his skin bounced back.

"Are you crazy?! Don't poke him, he might wake up!" Dr Michaels shouted in alarm.

Chemo did not move. None of the computer monitors changed. Dr Frank reached for a lab instrument. It looked like a shiny silver pencil connected to the wall by a thin tube.

"Let's see if I can make a small pin prick with this laser and drain off some of Chemo's liquid. If we're quick, it won't hurt him and shouldn't wake him up," Dr Frank said.
He pressed a small button on the instrument and the tube lit up. "Get ready with a sample jar, Dr Michaels."

HMMMMMMM!

The machine hummed. A bright white beam came out and hit Chemo's outer layer. A spot of white light spread out from where the beam touched Chemo's skin.

"It's not working. The laser isn't going through," Dr Michaels said as he stood next to Chemo with the sample jar.

"Let me switch over to the sonic setting," Dr Frank said.

SKREEE!

The laser hum turned into a high-pitched squeal.

"It's still not going through his skin, but . . . um . . . I think something else is happening," Dr Michaels said.

Tiny ripples formed in Chemo's liquid insides and spread out from where the instrument touched his outer layer. The two scientists watched as the small ripples turned into large rumbling waves that sloshed all through Chemo's body.

WUBBA! WUBBA! WUBBA!

"Oh no! The sound waves from the sonic setting are churning up Chemo's insides!" Dr Michaels said. "Turn it off!"

It was too late. All the sloshing had disturbed Chemo's calm. The monster suddenly woke up.

RAAAAR!

Chemo looked around wildly, clearly confused. He did not know where he was. The lights and sounds of this place were strange. He could not understand them. His first instinct was to get out of there, but when he tried to move he could not. Metal straps held him to a wall. Chemo pulled against them, but they were made of very thick metal and did not break. This made Chemo angry.

FWOOOSH!

Chemo was made of toxic chemicals. He shot a blast of them out of his mouthpiece. They landed on the metal straps.

SIZZZZLE!

The straps started to dissolve. Chemo pulled against the weakened restraints and broke them easily.

"He's loose!" Dr Frank yelled. "We have to get out of here!"

"Wait a sec! I can get a sample now!" Dr Michaels said. He grabbed a beaker and lunged towards Chemo's goo-covered straps.

"I don't know if you're brave or just crazy, but I don't want to find out," Dr Frank said as he grabbed Dr Michaels by the collar. Using all his strength, he dragged his partner out of the lab. As they passed through the door, he hit the emergency alarm.

WHOOOP! WHOOOP!

Loudspeakers blared. Lights flashed. Sirens sounded. The harsh sounds and lights upset Chemo. The high pitch of the sirens made his liquid insides vibrate. All he wanted to do was escape.

CRAAASH!

Chemo used his great strength and his metal fists to smash through one of the lab walls. Then the villain stomped through the hole and into the room next door. This one was as loud and confusing as the one he had just left.

SMAASH! SMAASH! SMAASH!

Chemo knocked down wall after wall, looking for a way to escape. Scientists fled in panic. More alarms went off. Chemo did not like the alarms. They hurt his insides.

Chemo did not know where he was going. He just kept moving forward because nothing in his way was strong enough to stop him.

THWUUUMP!

Suddenly, Chemo walked into something that *was* strong enough to stop him. To the villain it just looked like a blue and red man.

"Time to go back to sleep, Chemo," Superman said.

The Man of Steel gave Chemo a powerful punch that sent the creature flying back through all the holes in the walls he had smashed through. He ended up back in the lab where he had started his rampage.

WHUUUUMP!

Chemo hit a solid wall and slumped to the floor like a giant sack of gelatin. His insides sloshed back and forth with a gurgling sound.

Superman flew into the room and looked at all the damage. Smashed and ruined lab tables cluttered the floor. Electronic instruments sizzled and smoked. The straps that had once held the monster hissed as the toxic goo continued to melt them.

"You made quite a mess, Chemo," Superman said.

Chemo did not understand the words the blue and red man was saying. He only knew that the man had attacked him. This made Chemo angry.

RAAAAR!

CHAPTER 2

On a rampage

FWOOSH!

Chemo shot a blast of powerful chemicals at Superman. The liquid did not hurt the Man of Steel. It bounced off his body and splashed all over the lab.

HIIIISSS! Wherever goo hit, things started to dissolve.

I have to stop Chemo before he does any more damage, Superman thought.

The Man of Steel wrapped his arms around Chemo in a super-strong grip. To Chemo, it felt like the straps that had held him to the wall. He did not like that feeling. It added to his anger.

Chemo broke free from Superman's grasp. Even though Chemo was huge, he was fast. He whirled around and punched the Man of Steel with tremendous strength.

POWWWW!

The blow tossed Superman backwards. Free from his grip, Chemo smashed through another wall and lumbered away in the opposite direction.

"You're not going anywhere, Chemo," Superman said. The Man of Steel became a blur as he moved at super-speed. Suddenly he stood in front of Chemo, holding a giant spool of heavy metal cable in one hand.

Chemo's simple mind was confused. He had just left the strange blue and red man behind him. *FWHOOOSH!* Chemo gushed another stream of toxic goo at the man.

Superman quickly stepped aside from the gusher. Then he took the spool of cable and started to wrap it round and round the super-villain.

WHOOOSH! WHOOOSH! WHOOOSH!

It took only a few seconds for the creature to look like a caterpillar's cocoon. After that, Superman used his heat vision to melt the cable strands together. No matter how strong he was, Chemo could not snap them and break free.

"That should hold you," Superman said. "Now I need to repair the damage you've caused."

The Man of Steel looked around at the smashed walls and melting lab equipment. Sirens still shrieked. Bright red emergency lights flashed. But before Superman could start making repairs, he saw that the Chemo cocoon was melting from the inside out.

SIZZZZLE!

Toxic green goo dripped from the metal and onto the floor. The cement floor started to dissolve. Chemo burst free of the weakened cocoon. It fell at his feet.

The villain took out his anger on what was left of his former prison. *FWHOOSH!* He let loose with a gigantic gush of dangerous chemicals. The metal cocoon melted away and disappeared. So did the part of the floor Chemo stood on. A huge hole opened up to the level just below, and the enraged villain fell through it.

But Chemo did not stop there. He kept gushing chemicals and melted down through floor after floor.

Superman flew after Chemo. The hero landed in a large warehouse full of heavy machinery and huge trucks. A construction crane sat in the centre with a large container of blue liquid swinging from a heavy chain. The words "DANGER" and "HIGH EXPLOSIVES" were written on the sides of the container. People ran around the crane in a panic. Superman saw why – Chemo was stomping towards it.

I don't know what's in that container, but it's dangerous and I can't let Chemo get his hands on it, Superman thought.

Chemo didn't have real hands, but he clacked his robot claws as he marched towards the crane that held the container.

Superman zoomed up to Chemo and grabbed him by one of his claws. The Man of Steel lifted the villain off the ground before he could reach the crane and whirled him around and around. The motion made Chemo's liquid insides churn.

GLUUURGLE! GLUUURGLE!

Suddenly Superman let go of Chemo. The creature sailed across the huge room and hit the far wall. *BWHOOOMP!* This time Chemo bounced off the wall like a ball and zoomed back towards Superman. The Man of Steel flew up and out of the way, but then he saw that Chemo was shooting straight for the crane.

Superman moved with super-speed. He caught up with Chemo and shoved him away from the crane just in time. The creature managed to land on his feet.

Chemo skidded to a stop just before slamming into a line of large trucks parked in a row. The villain did not like being twirled and bounced and shoved around. Angry, he lifted the nearest truck and threw it at Superman.

"Temper, temper," the Man of Steel said as he caught the truck and put it gently on the ground.

Chemo tossed another large truck. Then another. He went down the line of parked vehicles and threw them one by one.

Superman easily caught them and gently set them back on the ground. Chemo grabbed the last truck in the row and lifted it over his head, ready to throw. But he did not aim at Superman. Chemo threw the truck at the crane.

CRAAASH!

The arm of the crane holding the container broke in half. The container fell to the ground and exploded.

BWOOOOM! The explosion set off other explosions in the warehouse. It started a chain reaction. Machinery blew up. Trucks blew up. Whatever was in the warehouse was in danger. Superman heard faint cries for help with his super-hearing. People were still in the warehouse. The Man of Steel used his X-ray vision to search for them.

WHOOOSH! WHOOOSH!

Superman found several workers and got them out of the warehouse at super-speed.

"Superman, you have to seal the warehouse," one of the workers said. "You can't let the explosions spread to the rest of S.T.A.R. Labs."

"I will, but I have to get Chemo out of there first," Superman said.

The Man of Steel zoomed at super-speed back into the warehouse. He searched through the smoke and noise for Chemo with his super-senses, but could not find the creature. The explosions got more and more intense.

At last Superman knew he had only a few more moments to save the rest of the S.T.A.R. Labs facility. He gripped the edges of the giant metal emergency doors and used his super-strength to pull them shut. Then he used his heat vision to seal them.

BLAAAAAAM!

The force of the final explosion shook the whole facility. The metal doors buckled slightly, but held.

Superman used his X-ray vision to look for Chemo one more time, but he could not see any trace of the creature.

"I wish I could have saved him," the Man of Steel said.

"Superman! We need your help!" someone shouted.

The hero turned his thoughts away from Chemo and raced to rescue the people still in danger.

CHAPTER 3

To the rescue

WHOOSH!

The force of the explosion launched Chemo skywards. The creature crashed through the ceiling of the warehouse and up through many levels of the underground S.T.A.R. Labs facility. He smashed through the last level and sailed out into the open air. After a while, Chemo landed with a squishy thud in the middle of a dense forest many kilometres away.

THWUUUMP! THWUUUMP! THWUUUMP!

Chemo bounced a few times and then rolled down a hillside like a runaway boulder. He did not try to stop as he smashed through the trees and brush. His liquid insides were so churned up that he had no idea what was happening.

At last the villain reached the bottom of the hill. The ground evened out and Chemo slowed down. When he finally came to a stop, he slowly pushed himself into a sitting position. He rested for a few minutes as his insides sloshed and gurgled.

BLAAARGH!

Chemo couldn't help but spew out some of his liquid. It landed on a clump of bushes and sizzled where the goo splattered on the leaves.

The forest was quiet around Chemo. The only sound was the gentle breeze passing through the tree branches. A bird chirped somewhere in the distance. No sirens shrieked. No lights flashed. The blue and red man was gone. Chemo felt calm for the first time since he woke up.

After a while, Chemo heard a sound that made him curious. It had a high pitch but it did not hurt him. Chemo did not recognize it. It sounded . . . happy . . . and it was coming from nearby.

Chemo got to his feet and lumbered off towards the sound of children laughing.

* * *

Superman zoomed through the S.T.A.R. Labs facility. He did all he could to help firefighters and other emergency crews.

The warehouse explosion had caused damage on almost every level. Walls had collapsed. People were trapped. Scientific equipment was destroyed.

The Man of Steel worked to get people out of the facility. He used his super-hearing to listen for faint calls for help. He could hear the smallest sound from the deepest part of the labs. As soon as he heard a cry for help, Superman used his X-ray vision to locate where it was coming from and find whoever was trapped.

"Help! I need help!" a weak voice gasped.

Superman heard the frail sound. He searched for its source with his X-ray vision. When he found it, he saw a scientist surrounded by fallen metal beams. They were the only things protecting him from the crumbling cement ceiling and walls.

ZOOOOOM! The Man of Steel raced at super-speed to rescue the scientist.

The hero dug through large chunks of cement to reach the man. Once he did, Superman saw that there was thick green goo all over the crumbling walls. It was dissolving the cement. This was what was making the walls fall, not damage from the explosion.

"This is the lab were Chemo started his rampage," Superman said. "What are you doing here?"

"I . . . I had to come back for a sample," Dr Michaels said. He clutched a small container of the green liquid. "If we know what Chemo is made from, we might be able to control him."

"It's too late for that," Superman said. "An explosion destroyed Chemo."

The scientist looked surprised, then his face turned sad.

"That's too bad. I had high hopes for what we could learn from Chemo," Dr Michaels said. "I didn't think anything could destroy the creature."

"It was a very big explosion," Superman replied.

CRUUUUMBLE!

Superman looked up to see the entire lab start to cave in. He grabbed Dr Michaels and punched a path to safety. The Man of Steel tunnelled up and out of the underground S.T.A.R. Labs facility. When he reached the surface, he saw a crowd of scientists and other workers. They had gathered to make sure everyone had got out and was safe. Superman landed with Dr Michaels.

"Dr Michaels! There you are!" Dr Frank shouted as he sprinted up to his partner. "I don't know if I should hug you or slap you for going back into that lab! It was a very dangerous thing to do."

"I know, but I was able to get the sample," Dr Michaels said and held up the small container of green goo. "Too bad it doesn't matter anymore. Superman says that Chemo was destroyed."

"Well, we can still use the sample to study his chemical make-up," Dr Frank said. "Something good might yet come out of it."

"Yes! It's able to melt through metal and concrete like a super-acid," Dr Michaels said. "We could develop it to cut through walls for emergency rescues."

"Good idea!" Dr Frank replied. The two scientists walked away in deep discussion.

Superman used his X-ray vision to make a final check of the S.T.A.R. Labs facility. The fires were put out. The underground structure was stable. All the people were safe. It was time for him to leave.

WHOOSH!

The Man of Steel launched into the sky. As he started to fly back to Metropolis, he noticed something strange. A trail of broken trees cut through the forest below him. It went straight down a hillside.

That doesn't look natural. I wonder what caused it, Superman thought.

The Man of Steel paused in mid-air and used his super-vision to look closer. Fresh sap dripped from the snapped branches. The soil was still damp around the roots of the uprooted trees.

This has just happened, Superman thought. *Did I miss another emergency while I was at S.T.A.R. Labs?*

He followed the path of damage down the hill. At last the Man of Steel reached a spot where the ground levelled off.

Whatever crashed through the forest stopped here, Superman thought. *But where is it now?*

A quiet, sizzling sound reached Superman's sensitive super-hearing. He searched for the source of the sound and found a puddle of green goo dissolving a clump of bushes.

That's some of Chemo's toxic chemicals! Superman thought. *He's alive! He must have survived the explosion, rolled down the hill and stopped here.*

The Man of Steel was about to use his super-vision to look for Chemo when he heard a high-pitched sound. At first Superman did not know what it was. A moment later another high-pitched squeal followed the first one. Now he knew exactly what it was.

Kids laughing, Superman thought. *If Chemo is alive and nearby, they could be in danger!*

CHAPTER 4

Calm before the storm

Superman leapt into the air and flew above the treetops. He followed the sound of children laughing and it led him to a large lake. The buildings of a summer camp stretched along the shore.

The Man of Steel used his telescopic vision to search for Chemo. He saw kids playing football in a large open field. Children paddled in canoes and swam in the lake. They sat at picnic tables making crafts or eating snacks. Everything looked very peaceful.

"I don't see Chemo. That's a relief," Superman said. "But he could still be around here somewhere."

The Man of Steel hovered in mid-air above the summer camp. He used his X-ray vision to search the thick forest. It was possible the trees could hide something as big as Chemo. All he could see were groups of hikers and their supervisors.

"Superman! Look! It's Superman!" came an excited shout from below.

One of the children had spotted the Man of Steel floating in the sky above the camp. The other children and their supervisors looked up quickly.

"Yay! Superman!"

"He came to visit us!"

"Hi, Superman!"

The kids jumped up and down as they cheered and waved at the Man of Steel. Most of them had never seen a super hero in person before.

Superman knew he could not stop looking for Chemo, but there was nothing wrong with taking a few moments to wave back.

The hero turned slowly in the air and waved at all the kids on the ground. When he waved down at the kids out on the lake, Superman noticed they were diving off a large, inflated platform.

From his place in the sky, the platform looked like a giant green pillow. Most of it was under the water when all the kids were piled on top of it. But as soon as they started jumping off, the rest of the float bobbed to the surface. Now Superman noticed that it

had a head, arms and legs.

"That's not a swimming platform," Superman realized. "That's Chemo!"

The hero did not know why Chemo was floating in the lake or why the creature did not react to a bunch of kids playing on top of him. But he did know that Chemo could turn violent at any moment.

ZOOOOM! The Man of Steel moved at super-speed. He took off his red cape and used it like a fish net to scoop up the kids swimming near Chemo. The children thought Superman was giving them a ride. They shouted with excitement.

"Wheeee!" they yelled.

Then Superman spotted several kids paddling in canoes near Chemo. He used his super-breath to create a bunch of small waves that gently pushed the canoes onto the beach.

Superman landed and let the kids out of his cape. Camp supervisors and even more children ran up and surrounded the Man of Steel.

"Please get everyone indoors," Superman told the supervisors. "It'll be safer there."

The adults were quick to realize that Superman meant that there was danger and he did not want to frighten the kids.

"I can't stay, but I'll come back after I finish my mission," Superman said.

"Awww," the kids moaned.

"Obey your supervisors," Superman said firmly as he flew into the sky.

The hero paused high in the air to make sure the kids were going inside the camp buildings. Then he zoomed down towards Chemo floating in the lake.

SPLAAASH! Superman plunged into the water not far from Chemo. He swam as fast as a torpedo and came up under the creature a few seconds later. The Man of Steel lifted him out of the water and flew away from the summer camp.

Chemo did not like being removed from the lake. His liquid insides were in balance with the still water. No sloshing or churning. Floating in it was peaceful. He had felt calm. Now he did not. Chemo reacted.

RAAAR! Chemo lashed out at whatever had taken him away from his peaceful surroundings. He opened his mouthpiece and let loose with a wide blast of toxic chemicals. Superman was underneath Chemo, so none of the goo reached him, but it did fall into the lake. A gentle current carried it towards a high-tech water treatment plant.

I can't let Chemo's toxic goo pollute the lake. That plant makes drinking water out of it, Superman thought. He used his heat vision to burn up the blobs of floating chemicals.

Chemo fought against the hold Superman had on him. The villain twisted and kicked and struck wildly with his fists. One lucky blow connected. It did not hurt Superman, but it did loosen his grip for a moment.

Chemo used his incredible strength to break free. As he started to fall, Superman flew after him. Chemo recognized the blue and red man who had bothered him before. *FWHOOOOSH!* Chemo spewed a flood of toxic chemicals at the Man of Steel.

The blast covered Superman with a thick

layer of green goo, but he ignored it. He reached out to grab the falling creature.

Chemo punched the annoying blue and red man. His metal fist hit super-hard skin.

CLAAANG!

Chemo felt the vibrations ripple through the liquid in his arm and chest. It spread all over his body. Chemo did not like the feeling.

Superman caught Chemo and stopped his fall. He held the villain in a super-tight grip around his arms and torso. Chemo hated that feeling. He struggled to be free.

SPLOOOOCH!

Suddenly, Superman felt Chemo slipping out of his grasp. The Man of Steel was covered in Chemo's slippery goo, but that wasn't why he could not hold onto the creature. Chemo stretched his upper body like a rubber band. It got thinner and thinner until it slid right out of Superman's grip.

"You're just full of surprises," Superman said as he watched Chemo plummet towards the lake.

BLAAAM! BWAAAM!

Suddenly a barrage of small missiles and other weapon fire streaked through the air. All of it was aimed at Chemo.

CHAPTER 5

Fire and fury

Superman was surprised to see missiles heading towards Chemo. He was even more surprised to see where they came from. A pair of military fighter jets zoomed through the sky. They fired more weapons as they approached the creature.

BLAAAAM! BWOOOM! BWAAAM!

The missiles exploded all around Chemo. A huge ball of flames surrounded the villain in mid-air.

Superman braced himself against the shock waves from the powerful explosions. The flames washed over him. He felt as if he was bathing in lava as the toxic goo burned away on his body.

Below the Man of Steel, the force of the explosions shook the forest. The water in the lake surged outwards in giant waves. One wave headed for the water treatment plant on the shore.

Superman swooped down towards the tremendous swell. He used his super-breath to blow a blast of cold air at the wave. It froze in an instant and created a huge wall of ice. The treatment plant was safe. Superman looked out over the lake. There was no sign of Chemo.

How did those fighter pilots know Chemo was here? Superman wondered.

"Superman!" a voice called up from the shore.

A military officer waved her arms at the Man of Steel to get his attention. The woman stood in the turret of an armoured Humvee. She wore a camo combat uniform and helmet. Her command Humvee was surrounded by a group of other military vehicles on the shore of the lake. The Man of Steel landed on the hood of the officer's command vehicle.

"Are you in charge of this operation?" Superman asked.

"Yes. I'm Major Boone," the officer replied. "My mission is to find and capture Chemo."

"How did you know that Chemo was still alive?" Superman asked. "Everyone thought he was destroyed in the S.T.A.R. Labs explosion."

"There was a bio-monitor on him," Major Boone said. "When it was still working after the explosion, S.T.A.R. Labs' scientists realized that Chemo had survived the blast. After that, they contacted us, and we tracked him here."

"If you wanted to capture him, why use missiles against him?" Superman asked.

"We were just trying to stun him," Major Boone replied. "It's too bad they destroyed him instead."

"I'm not so sure they did," Superman said.

"They created a very powerful explosion," the major said.

"So was the explosion at S.T.A.R. Labs," Superman replied. He looked around. "I can't see any trace of Chemo on the lake. At least not on the surface."

Superman rose into the air and hovered ten metres above the lake. He used his X-ray vision to look under the water. He saw a large shape sitting as still as a boulder on the bottom. But it was not a boulder. It was Chemo.

Why is Chemo just sitting there? Superman wondered. *Is he hurt? Did the missiles actually do some damage?*

The Man of Steel looked closer with his X-ray vision. He could not see any injury to Chemo's outer layer.

There must be something about being in the water that Chemo likes, Superman thought. *This is a clue to keeping him calm.*

Suddenly more missiles and rockets rained down on the lake from the military jets. They were aimed where Chemo was resting on the bottom.

Chemo's bio-monitor must still be working. Major Boone is using it to target him, Superman realized.

BLAAAM! BAAAM! BOOOM!

The weapons exploded underwater and just above the surface. The lake water churned all around the villain. Chemo's insides started churning too. He did not like the feeling at all. He got to his feet and started to move.

Superman watched with his X-ray vision as Chemo walked along the bottom of the lake. He headed for shore and the military vehicles.

"Chemo's alive and coming your way," Superman shouted to Major Boone.

"I know," the officer shouted back. "We're tracking his movements."

A moment later Chemo lumbered out of the water. The first thing he saw was a line of armoured vehicles roaring through the forest towards him. The engines were very loud. Then the vehicles started firing energy cannons at him.

FZZZZT! FZZZZT! FZZZZT!

The blasts bounced off Chemo's thick skin. None of them actually hurt the villain, but the noise and vibration they caused upset his liquid insides. This made him angry.

RAAAR!

Chemo aimed a wide blast of toxic chemicals at the military vehicles. They were quickly covered in thick green goo and started to melt. The soldiers leapt to safety just in time.

VROOOM!

Major Boone stood in her turret as her command Humvee drove towards Chemo at full speed. She ordered her driver to put the vehicle between Chemo and her soldiers. She looked down the barrel of her energy cannon at the giant green menace. Chemo stomped towards the major's Humvee.

"Wait!" Superman shouted.

The Man of Steel swooped down. His eyes burned red as he fired his heat vision. Twin beams of super-hot energy hit one of the empty armored vehicles that was already half-melted by Chemo's toxic goo. Superman melted it the rest of the way and turned it into a big blob of molten metal.

The hero lifted the blob in one hand. Then he picked up a second vehicle with his other hand. He aimed his heat vision at it and turned it into another glob of red-hot metal.

With two molten globs in hand, the Man of Steel zoomed towards Chemo.

SPLOOOOSH!

He clapped his handfuls of melted metal around the creature. Chemo was instantly encased in a ball of super-hot goo.

FWHOOOSH!

Superman blew a blast of cold air on the hot blob. It hardened instantly.

"If Chemo can survive all those powerful explosions, he'll survive inside a ball of metal," Superman said.

The Man of Steel took the Chemo ball and flew at super-speed into the sky. He did not stop until he left the Earth's atmosphere. At last Superman was beyond the planet's gravity. He let go of the metal ball and let it drift towards the stars.

This isn't the bottom of a lake, but I hope it's nice and quiet up here for you, Superman thought as he watched the ball float away. Then he turned and flew back towards Earth.

Inside the ball, Chemo was calm at last. His liquid interior started to slowly freeze in the super-cold of space. His mind slowed, as if it was drifting into hibernation. He felt a dim sense of happiness at finding some peace and quiet at last.

Chemo

NAME: Chemo (KEH-mo)

SPECIES: Monster

BASE: Mobile

HEIGHT: 7.6 metres

WEIGHT: 2,584 kilograms

EYES: Yellow

HAIR: None

POWERS/ABILITIES: Superhuman strength and durability. Chemo also has the ability to regenerate himself, change his size and shape, and spew highly toxic and radioactive chemicals at his foes.

BIOGRAPHY:

Chemo's origin stems from rather humble beginnings. Before coming to life, Chemo was simply the nickname of a man-shaped plastic container in scientist Ramsey Norton's lab. Whenever Norton had a failed experiment, he would dump the resulting chemical compounds into Chemo for storage. One fateful day, however, disaster struck. Norton added the by-products of a failed growth formula to Chemo, and the container of toxic soup stirred to life. Enraged and confused, Chemo erupted into a radioactive rampage that killed Norton and allowed the villain to escape the lab.

- As a container of chemicals brought to life, Chemo is not known for his intelligence. But what he lacks in brains, he definitely makes up for in brawn. The villain loves nothing more than destroying things. He packs punches and hurls heavy equipment with devastating results. And the radioactive chemicals he spews cut through concrete and melt metal into molten sludge with ease.

- Chemo was originally an enemy of the Metal Men. This team of liquid metal robot super heroes, created by brilliant scientist Doc Magnus, fought and destroyed the radioactive super-villain many times. However, Chemo's strange brew of powers allowed him to re-form every time.

- Through the years, Chemo has been known to join forces with criminal organizations such as the Injustice League, the Secret Society of Super-Villains and the Suicide Squad. While these team-ups often place Chemo squarely in Superman's sights, the hero's powers largely protect him from the toxic troublemaker.

BIOGRAPHIES

Author

Laurie S. Sutton has been reading comics since she was a kid. She grew up to become an editor for Marvel, DC Comics, Starblaze and Tekno Comics. She has written Adam Strange for DC, Star Trek: Voyager for Marvel, plus Star Trek: Deep Space Nine and Witch Hunter for Malibu Comics. There are boxes of comics in her wardrobe instead of clothing and shoes. Laurie has lived all over the world and currently resides in Florida, USA.

Illustrator

Leonel Castellani has worked as a comic artist and illustrator for more than twenty years. Mostly known for his work on licensed art for companies such as Warner Bros., DC Comics, Disney, Marvel Entertainment and Cartoon Network, Leonel has also built a career as a conceptual designer and storyboard artist for video games, movies and TV. In addition to drawing, Leonel also likes to sculpt and paint. He currently lives in La Plata City, Argentina.

GLOSSARY

antidote a substance that stops a poison from working

bio-monitor a device that keeps track of someone's life signs

dissolve to disappear into something else

gelatin a clear substance used in making jelly, desserts and glue

hibernation a resting state used to survive poor conditions in the environment

instinct behaviour that is natural rather than learned

radioactive having to do with materials that give off potentially harmful invisible rays or particles

restraint a bar, strap, chain or other object that holds someone still

toxic poisonous

vibration a fast movement back and forth

DISCUSSION QUESTIONS

1. When the scientists try to take a sample from Chemo, the villain erupts in a rage. Who do you feel more sorry for when this happens – Chemo or the scientists? Discuss why you feel the way you do.

2. When Superman finds Chemo at the summer camp, the villain appears to be at peace. Chemo even lets the children use him as a float. Why do you think he is so calm in this situation?

3. Throughout the story, Chemo tries to find somewhere he can enjoy peace and quiet. Where do you like to go when you need to calm down or relax? Why?

WRITING PROMPTS

1. Make a list of the powers Superman uses during his battles with Chemo. Then pick one of those powers and write a short paragraph explaining why you would like to have it.

2. When Superman arrives at the lake, he finds children playing on Chemo. But how did that happen? Write a scene that shows how Chemo arrived near the camp and explains why the children start using him as a float.

3. At the end of the story, Superman encases Chemo in a ball of molten metal and sets the villain adrift in space. How do you think he escapes? Write a new chapter that describes how Chemo escapes, where he goes and what he does next.